Waybuloo

Nok Tok
Goes Driving

First published in Great Britain 2009 by Egmont UK Limited
239 Kensington High Street, London W8 6SA
Waybuloo ™ & © 2009 The Foundation
TV Productions Limited/Decode/Blue Entertainment.
Licensed by RDF Rights. All rights reserved.
With the support of the MEDIA Programme of the European Union

rdf rights
part of the rdf media group

MEDIA

ISBN 978 1 4052 4753 5
1 3 5 7 9 10 8 6 4 2
Printed in Italy

One day in Nara, Nok Tok visits De Li in her garden. She is making a rockery, but she has a problem.

"Need one more rock," says De Li.

Nok Tok always likes to help his friends. **"Nok Tok find rock for De Li,"** he offers.

"Thank you, Nok Tok," she smiles.

Nok Tok looks for the perfect rock for De Li. He finds one that's big and round.

"Found rock!" he cheers.

Nok Tok lifts up the rock. It's very heavy!

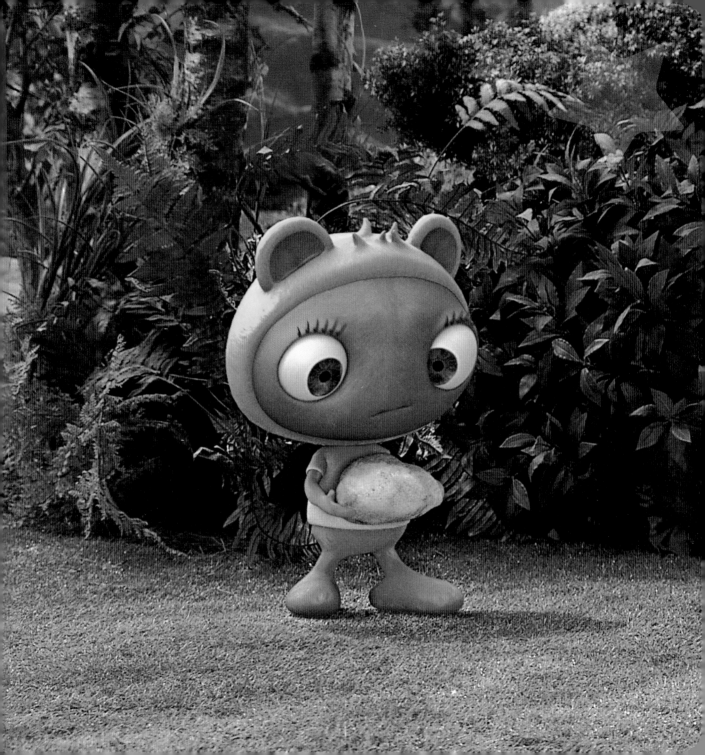

Nok Tok sees Yojojo carrying a bamboo pole. But it's too heavy for Yojojo!

"Nok Tok carry bamboo for Yojojo," says Nok Tok.

"Thank you, Nok Tok!" Yojojo calls happily as he bounces away.

Nok Tok lifts up the rock and the pole. They are both heavy, but Nok Tok is strong.

"Never give up!" Nok Tok says to himself.

Lau Lau wants to move a stone statue to her home. She pulls as hard as she can, but it's just too heavy!

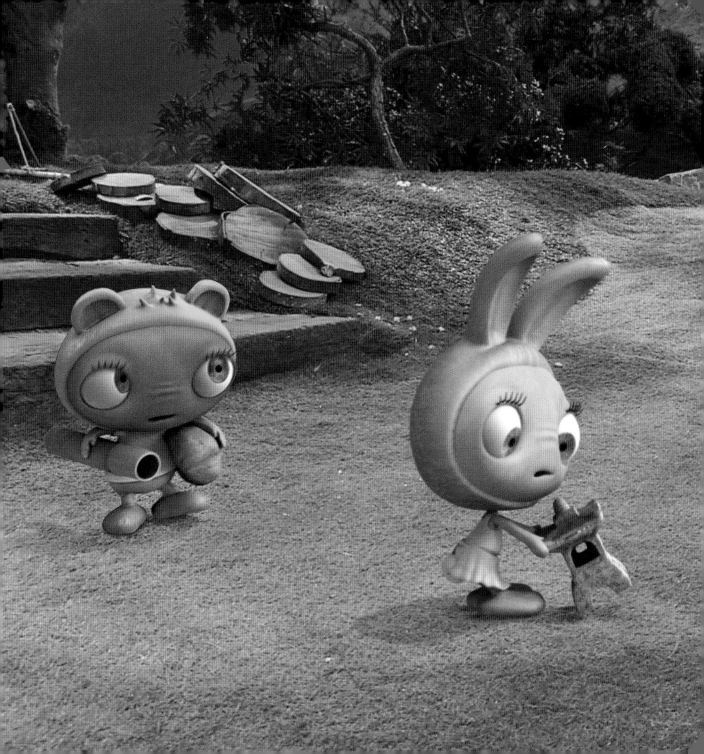

Nok Tok puts down his things and goes over to Lau Lau. He wants to help his friend.

"Nok Tok help Lau Lau," he offers.

"Thank you, Nok Tok!" smiles Lau Lau as she hops away.

Nok Tok lifts the rock in one hand and the pole in his other hand. But now he can't carry the statue because his hands are full!

Just then, Nok Tok hears the cheebies laughing.

"Let's play peeka!" he calls excitedly. He can help his friends later!

Yojojo and Lau Lau hide in a tree.

De Li hides under a big leaf.

And Nok Tok hides behind a rock!

The cheebies find the Piplings one by one.

"Found you!" they all cheer happily.

After peeka, Nok Tok wants to finish helping his friends. But how can he carry all the heavy things?

"Train!" he hears near by. The cheebies make a train by holding on to each other as they walk.

"Thinkapow!" Nok Tok has an idea!

"Cheebies help Nok Tok?" he asks, and they all say yes! He whispers his idea to them, and they soon gather everything he needs.

"Thank you, cheebies!" says Nok Tok. He goes into his workshop and uses his Pipling tools.

Bang! Clang! Clunk!

"Finished!" smiles Nok Tok. He gathers everyone together to show them his special surprise.

"Nok Tok make car to help Piplings!" he announces.

He puts the heavy things in the car and jumps in, too. When the wind blows on the leaf, the car begins to move – just like a sailing boat!

The Piplings clap and cheer as Nok Tok delivers the rock, the pole, and the statue to their homes.

"Thank you, Nok Tok!" they say happily when he has finished.

Nok Tok is so pleased to help his friends that he floats into the air.

"Buloo!" he smiles.

De Li, Yojojo and Lau Lau float up into the air too. **"Waybuloo!"** they say together as they loop and glide in the sky.

"Bye bye, cheebies. See you next time!"